This
Ready

book i

My Reading Tree!

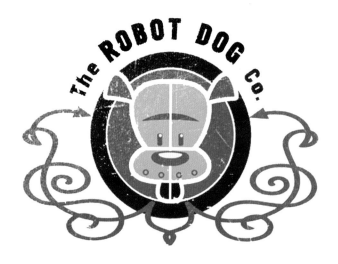

To my very own
'Scrap', Lorcan
— M. O.

LITTLE TIGER PRESS
An imprint of Magi Publications
1 The Coda Centre, 189 Munster Road, London SW6 6AW
www.littletigerpress.com

First published in Great Britain 2005
by Little Tiger Press, London
This edition published 2011

Text and illustrations copyright © Mark Oliver 2005

Printed in China
LTP/1800/0261/0611
ISBN 978-1-84895-359-8
2 4 6 8 10 9 7 5 3 1

ROBOT DOG

MARK OLIVER

LITTLE TIGER PRESS

In a factory, on a hill,
a huge machine made
robot dogs.

The robot dogs rolled out of
the factory and were delivered to
owners who played with them and
loved them and cared for them.

The dogs were very happy
because all dogs, even robot
dogs, want an owner.

One little dog on the conveyor belt was very excited.

"I wonder what my owner will be like," he said. "What will I be called?"

He was much too excited to sit still—he jumped and frolicked and bounced up and down.

But then, CRASH! He bounced too high and clonked his ear. Suddenly, alarm bells rang, red lights flashed, and a cloud of smoke whooshed as the huge machine ground slowly to a stop.

The machine
inspected the
robot dog very
carefully. Finally,
a voice boomed:

"NOT RUSTY OR DUSTY,
NOT BATTERED OR BENT,
NO PATCHES OR SCRATCHES,
BUT THERE IS A DENT!

SCRAP!"

"So that's my name!"
thought Scrap as the
machine picked him
up and dropped him
through a hatch.

Scrap slid down a chute
and landed in a yard full of junk.
   There, staring at him, were
some other dogs.
   "Hello!" he said. "I'm Scrap!
Where am I? Where's my owner?"
   One of the dogs said, "You don't
have an owner—you're a reject like us."

Bumper, Dent, Scratch, and Sniffer
all lived in the yard. It was
a wonderful place to play,
just a bit messy, the
way dogs like it.

They often played with other dogs
who had owners. But sooner
or later their owners
would call:
 "Come on, Shiny!"
 "Dinner time, Sparkle!"

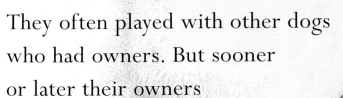

Then they stopped
 whatever they were
 doing and ran home.
  Seeing the other dogs
 go off happily to their
 owners made the yard
 dogs feel a bit sad.

"Why don't we get an owner?"
said Scrap one day.

"They take a lot of looking after,"
replied Bumper. "They like things to be
tidy, and you need to play games and fuss
over them to keep them happy."

But the more they all talked about it,
the more they *really* wanted an owner.

"How can we get one?" said Sniffer.
"We're rejects!"

"There must be a way," thought Scrap.

As Scrap started thinking, the cogs in his brain started turning. They went around faster and faster as he thought harder and harder. Finally, a light flickered on!

"I've got an idea!" Scrap announced to the other dogs, excitedly. "Come and help me!"

The dogs raced around collecting
anything that might be useful.

They worked all day and all night, and by the next morning the dogs were exhausted, but very proud, because . . .

. . . there stood an owner!

He was rusty and dusty, battered and bent, patched, scratched, and covered in dents—but he had a heart of gold.

Their owner played with
them and loved them and
cared for them. And the dogs
were very happy, because
all dogs, even robot dogs,
want an owner.

Time to Rhyme!

Words that have the same sounds as one another are called **rhyming words**. E.g. back – pack. Match each word below with the word sticker it rhymes with.

1) dog   _____

2) scrap   _____

3) proud   _____

4) play   _____

5) rusty   _____

6) yard   _____

 Did you match the rhyming words?
Then add a star to your reading tree!

Picture Dictionary

Look at the words below and put the correct
picture sticker next to each word.

house   tire

wrench   mouse

Did you get these right? Remember to
add another star to your reading tree!

Past Tense

A **verb** is an action word. If a verb describes something
that has already happened, it is in the **past tense**.
Some verbs end in **-ed** to show that they are in the past tense.
Look at the sentences below and underline
the verbs in the past tense.

1) The machine inspected the robot dog very carefully.

2) "They take a lot of looking after," replied Bumper.

3) Finally, a light flickered on.

4) Their owner played with them and loved them and
cared for them.

Did you find the past tense verbs?
Add another star to your reading tree!

Lost Letters!

Oh, no! Some of the letters in the words from the story have disappeared. Write the missing letter in each word, using the letters from the box.

> a – e – i – o – u

> 1) d_nner 2) _wners 3) m_ssy
> 4) d_sty 5) h_ppy

Did you spell the words right? Don't forget to add another star to your reading tree!

Crazy Capitals

A sentence always begins with a **capital letter**.
E.g. **W**here's my owner?
Capital letters are also used for names of people and places.
E.g. **C**ome on, **S**hiny!
Look at the sentences below.
Circle the letters that should be capitals.

> 1) one little dog on the conveyor belt was very excited.
> 2) scrap slid down a chute and landed in a yard full of junk.
> 3) bumper, dent, scratch, and sniffer all lived in the yard.
> 4) they often played with the other dogs who had owners.

Did you circle all the capital letters?
Put another star on your reading tree!

Rhythmic Syllables

Every word is made up of one or more **syllables**. A word that is one beat long has one syllable, like "dog". A word that is two beats long has two syllables, like "rusty" (rus + ty). A word that is three beats long has three syllables, like "exhausted" (ex + haus + ted).

Read out the words below. Count the syllables in each word and put the sticker with the correct number of syllables next to each word.

1) factory   (3 syllables)
_____

2) junk
_____

3) robot
_____

4) bent
_____

5) faster
_____

6) happily
_____

Did you get the syllables right?
Add a star to your reading tree!

Simple Sentences

These sentences from the story have been split in the middle and mixed up! Draw a line to join them up again. We've done the first one for you.

1) In a factory, on a hill,

and ran home.

2) Then they stopped whatever they were doing

because all dogs, even robot dogs, want an owner.

3) "How can we get one?"

a huge machine made robot dogs.

4) "I've got an idea!"

said Sniffer.

5) And the dogs were very happy,

Scrap announced to the other dogs, excitedly.

Did you get this right? Remember to add the last star to your reading tree!